JUNGLE JAMBOREE

Jo Empson

For John & Sophie,
with endless love

PUFFIN BOOKS

UK | USA | Canada | Ireland | Australia
| India | New Zealand | South Africa

Puffin Books is part of the Penguin Random House group of companies
whose addresses can be found at global.penguinrandomhouse.com.

www.penguin.co.uk   www.puffin.co.uk   www.ladybird.co.uk

Penguin
Random House
UK

First published 2019
001

Printed in China
A CIP catalogue record for this book is available from the British Library

ISBN: 978-0-141-35689-1

All correspondence to:
Puffin Books, Penguin Random House Children's
80 Strand, London WC2R 0RL

FSC
www.fsc.org

MIX
Paper from
responsible sources
FSC® C018179

Deep in the jungle, the beat of the drums
spoke of a grand event.
A chitter-chatter swept through the treetops
and the word soon spread . . .

A jungle jamboree!

Tonight at dusk.

All creatures welcome, great and small.

But who will be the **most beautiful** of all?

"Not me!" roared the lion.
"My mane is . . .

too

dull!"

"Not me!"
chirped the bird.
"My legs
are too
short!"

"Not me!" snorted the zebra.
"My stripes are too **boring!**"

"Not me!" whispered the leopard.
"My spots are far too spotty!"

"Not me!"
sighed the hippo.
"My bottom is . . .

too

BIG

"I wonder what's for lunch," said the fly, who just flew on by.

All the creatures disappeared
into the jungle to get ready
for the jamboree . . .

. . . all apart from the **fly**,
who happily ate his lunch,
enjoying the beautiful view

without a worry in the world.

Finally all the creatures were ready.
But somehow they didn't quite look themselves.
Something had changed . . .

"Surely now I will be
the most beautiful of all,"
purred the lion,
flicking his
feathery mane.

"Easily me!"
sang
the
bird
with
lovely
long
bamboo
legs.

"Definitely me!"

laughed
the zebra,
giving a
**colourful
twirl.**

"Clearly me, "

secretly thought the leopard,
all **spotless** and **flowery**.

"Ta-da! Obviously me . . ."

announced the hippo with her fancy pants!

"What a **beautiful** end to the day," said the fly.

As the sun grew weary and rested
upon the hill, dusk fell
over the jungle – it was time
for the jungle jamboree!

All the creatures gathered,
great and **small**,
along with the judges to decide
who would be crowned
the **most beautiful** of **all.**

But the clouds were not tired
and wanted to have some fun.

So they whipped up a storm,
causing mischief
and chaos . . .

. . . blowing and washing away

all the fancy frills!

"Oh no! My feathery mane!" roared the lion.

"Nooo! My fancy pants!" cried the hippo.

At last the clouds grew tired

and put their mischief to bed.
But darkness had fallen upon the jungle.

The judges could not see who deserved
to be crowned the most
beautiful of all.

"Let me give you all
some light," said the fly.

Zipping all around, the light
of the **firefly** shone brightly,
showing the judges
the creatures' natural beauty.

"You **all** look **so** beautiful," said the judges,
"just as you are!"

But everyone agreed . . .

. . . the firefly's kindness was the most
beautiful thing of all!

"I wonder what's for supper," said the fly.

And home he flew.